Gravespeakers: Maria

ANTHONY GARVEY

ISBN-13:978-1530690879

DEDICATION

To Siobhán for sticking with me through thin and thin.

To Zach and Samuel, for being the inspiration for this entire book series.

To Ruth, Aileen, Mike, Grace, Lauren, Ciara, Liam, Megan, Joyce, Andrew, Claire, Bren and Luc for listening to and helping with endless drafts.

And to every school and pupil I have visited offering advice, encouragement and cups of hot lemon.

Remember – come to the edge!

Thank you all!

Chapter One

"I keep having the same dream."

Twelve-year-old Maria Lyons brushed her straight, black hair in long, even strokes. She peered over at her best friend Helen, who was sitting uneasily on a rickety chair in Maria's bedroom.

"Standing beside my wardrobe every night is a dead person, eyes and mouth sealed shut, their hands reaching out towards me. They stay for two nights and then they are gone, replaced by new people who have recently died."

"Oh my God, what a horrible dream," Helen spluttered, her hands clasped tightly together. "Aren't you frightened?"

Maria shook her head.

"I spend my whole life surrounded by death, so why should it be any different when I'm asleep? Besides real life is a lot scarier."

Maria put her hairbrush down and started to tidy up her bedside locker.

After a few moments Helen asked softly:

"Did you know any of the dead people?"

"Dad looked after them all," Maria replied casually, tugging gently on the locket round her neck. "Last month it was Dougal, the man from the park. Dougal had drunk so much alcohol, Dad said he didn't need any for the embalming. Last week it was John, our old postman."

"You have an over-active imagination and who could blame you?" Helen declared, waving her hands dismissively.

"Living across the road from a graveyard has got to mess with your head, but you must be the only girl in Ireland who has fresh wreaths in her bedroom."

"I don't mind. Dad doesn't have space for them downstairs."

"Why," Helen began slowly, almost as if she didn't want to ask the next question. "How long have you been having this dream?"

"Since I was seven."

"Since you were WHAT?" Helen said, wrinkles of astonishment crisscrossing her forehead. "How could you keep this a secret for five years?"

"I told dad when it happened first. He said I had a gift."

"What a wonderful way to comfort a seven-year-old child," Helen said sarcastically.

"Dad taught me there's nothing to fear because the dead can't harm you. He was right in a way about it being a gift. It can be reassuring. I got to see Auntie Annie after she passed away and then of course," Maria added falteringly, "there was mum."

"It would freak me out," Helen gasped, beads of sweat appearing near her forehead. "I don't know how you can be so cool about it."

"I've got used to it by now," Maria replied, looking down at her hard hands with her soft blue eyes. "I've even put up some posters so I can look at my favourite bands instead of dead people wiggling their hands at me."

Helen shook her mousy brown hair vigorously. She got to her feet, pulled back the curtains and opened the window.

As the fresh air streamed into the bedroom, Helen glanced up at the cold, imposing church across the road. The sun was going down and in the graveyard beside the church Maria's father was busy digging.

2

"Your dad's nearly finished Paul Browne's grave."

Helen paused for a moment, as if weighing up the evidence.

"Are you saying Paul Browne will be standing by your wardrobe in his smelly wellies tonight?" Helen asked.

"He's already checked in, arrived last night," Maria replied.

Helen shook her head.

"It's just a dream though isn't it?" Helen insisted.

Maria said nothing, so Helen tried a different approach.

"So if the dream doesn't bother you, why are you telling me about it at all?"

Maria leaned forward excitedly:

"Last night was different. Paul Browne was standing in exactly the same spot as they normally do, but this time his eyes were open."

"Ooooh spooky!" Helen replied, her breathing getting a little faster again. "Are you sure it wasn't the light from the moon playing tricks on you?"

"A blue light burned in his eyes and his mouth was open, but there's more," Maria whispered. "He spoke to me."

"What did he say?"

"Just two words."

Maria spoke in a deep, gravelly voice: "*HELP ME*."

End Chapter One

Chapter Two

"I like your haircut Vinnie," Helen said, plonking her schoolbag down beside her desk in Tarbert National School.

"I asked them for a surfer dude meets Indy kid cut!" Vinnie replied, his deep brown eyes sparkling with delight, as he ran his fingers through his wavy chestnut hair. "Worked out really well. How was Maria last night?"

"I'm worried about her," said Helen. "Did she tell you about her dream?"

Vinnie shook his head.

"Maria's been seeing dead people."

"Has she been watching that scary film with Bruce Willis?"

"She claims dead people are standing at the end of her bed with their eyes closed, wiggling their hands at her."

Vinnie looked over his shoulder.

"Sounds like Colin during Maths class."

"Will you take this seriously?" Helen implored. "Maria claims she has been having these dreams for five years. I thought she might have told you about it?"

"I haven't heard anything. If it makes you feel any better, I'll have a word with her later."

Moments later Maria arrived in class. Helen put her finger to her lips and took the seat beside her. Their teacher Ms Kearns, a young woman in her early 20s, strode into the classroom.

"Now settle down everyone," Ms Kearns said. "I know it's Friday and next week is our last week at school before the Summer holidays..."

All the children cheered.

"But, but, before we go, there are one or two more topics I'd like to cover."

Over the next hour Ms Kearns talked about modern art and the paintings she had seen when she was a student in America. She showed the children three images of famous paintings using the overhead projector.

"I got to see these paintings every day when I worked during the summer in the Museum of Modern Art in New York," Ms Kearns said, her chest puffing out with pride. "The first is 'Starry Night' by Van Gogh."

"Those stars look weird," said Paula, a tall wiry girl at the back of the class.

"Why is there a mountain at the front?" asked Susie, a petite girl with a heavily freckled face.

"It looks to me like a big black tree," Helen suggested.

"This was painted not at night, but during the day from Van Gogh's memory of the night sky," Ms Kearns informed the children.

"Well his memory is wonky," Paula replied. "Someone needs to tell him stars have six points. His have none."

The next painting the children got to see was 'I and the Village' by Marc Chagall.

"I like the ponies and faces, it's a happy painting," said Lucy, a well-built girl with glasses, sitting near the front of the class.

"Why is the woman upside down?" asked Erica, a girl with braces sitting next to Lucy.

"Because she's about to be killed dumbo," said Mark, a large boy, sitting on his own at the back of the class.

"I don't like the green face in the picture," said Colin. "It looks like someone is sick."

"The final painting I want to show you today is the 'Persistence of Memory' by Salvador Dali. Dali was a surrealist and this is my favourite painting in the whole Museum. What do you see in it?"

"Those clocks are rubbish. Only one of them looks real and it is set to the time I hate most. Five to seven in the morning, when I have to get up for school. Yuck!" Paula said and the children laughed.

"Is that an animal in the middle?" asked Lucy.

"I think it's a bent face," Colin replied. "Are those ants running up and down the watch?"

Maria who had been daydreaming suddenly took a keen interest in this picture. Her excitement spilled over and without realising it she blurted out one single word: 'cheese'.

Some of the children laughed and Mark shouted the word 'weirdo', but Ms Kearns asked the class to be quiet for a moment.

"What made you think of cheese?" Ms Kearns asked Maria.

"It's got something to do with the reason it was painted," Maria said. "I can't explain why, but I feel it."

"Well children, instead of laughing at Maria, you should be applauding her for being so perceptive. One night Dali and his wife had some guests round for supper and offered them wine and Camembert cheese."

"I'd go home if someone offered me wine and cheese," Paula piped up.

"Dali fell asleep and when he woke, the cheese had melted. He was still dazed from his sleep and to him, the clock seemed to be moving slowly. So looking at the cheese again, Dali had the idea time was melting and he decided to start painting."

"Another weirdo," said Mark.

"He worked all day to finish it and when he had done so, he asked his wife just one question: 'How soon will you forget this painting?'

'No one who sees it, will forget it' she said, which is the real power of the picture."

At break time Helen and Vinnie went over to talk to Maria.

"I've had it with Mark Mullins," Maria grumbled. "He's been picking on us all year. It doesn't normally bother me when people laugh and jeer at me – it's been happening to me since I was five – but everybody has a breaking point."

"Don't let it bother you," said Vinnie. "They've been calling me moneybags since I started coming to school and I just ignore it. Besides there's only a week left and we're out of here."

"That's not the point," Maria said. "Somebody needs to teach him a lesson."

"Vinnie are you going anywhere exotic for your Summer holidays?" Helen asked, quickly changing the subject.

"My parents are skiing for four weeks on Blackcomb Mountain above Whistler."

"Where?"

"It's near Vancouver in Canada. My dad says I need another year practising on the bunnies before I can get waist-deep in powder on the black diamond runs."

"I'm guessing you mean you're not quite a good enough skier yet," Helen smiled.

"Next year when I go, I can do mountain-biking, zip-lining, kayaking, fly-fishing and bear spotting."

"Bear spotting?"

"Vancouver's full of bears – grizzlies and black bears. If you are careful, dad says, it's a great experience."

Helen was about to say something when Mark appeared in the schoolyard. Maria rose to her feet.

"Mark," she called in her loudest voice. "I want a word with you."

Mark licked his lips and strolled casually over. He towered above Maria and many of the other children began to gather around.

"What do you want weirdo?" he snarled, spitting at her with contempt.

"I want three things. I want you to stop calling me weirdo. I want you to listen to other people respectfully when they are talking in class. And I want you to stop bullying children in school starting NOW!"

Helen and Vinnie looked on in amazement.

Mark moved closer to Maria and leaned over her:

"Nobody tells me what to do," he said menacingly. "I do what I like and I like what I do. What's a pipsqueak like you going to do to stop me?" he said.

"My dad Spencer taught me everything he knows about the funeral business," Maria said calmly. "If you don't stop bullying people right now, I will visit you one night when you are asleep. I'll stitch up your eyes and sew your big mouth shut. Just one more case of bullying is all it will take and I will come for you. Now push off before I get really angry," she said, turning back towards her friends.

The children who had gathered spontaneously gave Maria a round of applause and Mark snorted to himself as he pushed his way back through them.

***

As Maria was putting dinner on the table that evening, her father was getting changed out of his black suit. He always kept a shirt and tie on in case anyone called to the house. Maria had got a nice bit of lamb from O' Donnell's, added a few vegetables and potatoes and made a casserole. While the food was cooking, she was working on a school project. Her father said grace and they ate together in silence. Afterwards Maria made a pot of tea and poured her father a cup.

"I'm working on a science project to prove I can make raisins swim up and down inside a jam jar. I need little vinegar and baking soda and..."

Maria stopped mid-sentence, her father was looking distractedly out the window.

"Dad," Maria said falteringly. "Can I ask you a question?"

"Hmm," her father replied.

"Do you love me?"

After a few seconds her father rose from the table.

"Don't ask silly questions," he snapped. "Get the dishes done and finish off your homework. I have work to do."

End Chapter Two

Chapter Three

On Saturday morning Maria was winding a length of ribbon round a wreath in soft curls when a woman in her early 30s, marched into the funeral home. The woman's narrow-set eyes were red and her thin lips blue, the same colour as the striking drop pendant round her elegant neck.

"Deirdre Browne isn't it?" said Spencer Lyons, as he stepped from behind the counter to shake her hand. "I'm sorry for your loss. If it's any consolation, your father passed away peacefully in his sleep."

She was wearing an oversized woollen cardigan and Maria thought the stonewashed skinny jeans she had on went with her leather ankle boots perfectly.

Deirdre took out a cigarette and lit it up.

"I'm afraid we have a no smoking policy here," Spencer said softly.

Inhaling deeply on the cigarette, Deirdre blew the smoke into Spencer's face. Undaunted, he held up an ashtray and the young woman snorted as she stubbed the cigarette out.

"The last time I saw you was on your 18th birthday when you left Tarbert to go to America," Spencer continued, without losing his composure. "When did you arrive back?"

"Yesterday," Deirdre replied curtly.

"In your absence we've made the funeral arrangements. We put the obituary notice in the papers and let the people of the village know your father was reposing with us here. Do you want to see him?" Spencer asked, gesturing towards a room in the funeral home.

"What for? He's dead, isn't he?"

"Sometimes it can be comforting to see a loved one at a time of great loss."

Deirdre's cheeks reddened for a moment.

"I'll speak plainly, so we understand each other. My father and I weren't close and I don't want to be here any longer than I need to be. I'm his only child, so I've put the farm up for sale, but there's one small problem I still have to resolve."

Maria's ears pricked up as she adjusted the leaves and flower stems in the wreath, so they were pointing in the same direction.

"I don't know where my father kept his money. He didn't have a bank account and he paid for everything in cash. I spent yesterday on my hands and knees searching the farmhouse from top to bottom, but I still couldn't find it."

"Perhaps you'll get a chance to see your father at the removal later this evening," Spencer continued, unabashed.

"Is all this absolutely necessary?"

"It is traditional and we have put notices in the local papers and on Radio Kerry. Some people prefer to have a wake in their house, but most choose a viewing here in the funeral home. It gives the people of the village a chance to pay their respects. And many of your father's old friends, who knew him well, will be coming to say goodbye."

"Right, I hear what you are saying," Deirdre said slowly, considering Spencer's words. "His friends would know his little habits better than anyone, wouldn't they? I might shake a few hands before I fly home," Deirdre said, turning tail and slamming the door of the funeral home behind her.

Three hours later the people of the village began to arrive to pay their respects. Mr Browne's extended family was sitting together in a wide circle.

Some were crying softly, others had their heads bowed and in the middle was Deirdre, checking emails on her mobile. As the first of the villagers filed in, she hurriedly put her phone back in her handbag.

Mr Browne was in the centre of the room in an open casket, his hands and head visible, his lower body covered in a shroud. He wore a fresh shirt and a dark blue suit and he was clean shaven.

Maria stood at the front door and greeted the people from the village as they came in. Her father was an equal distance between the coffin and the members of the family, so he could deal with any issues which might arise. Villager after villager shook hands with members of the family saying how sorry they were for their troubles. 'He'll be sorely missed', 'he was greatly loved', 'there won't be another like him', were greeted by Deirdre with the same half smile.

"Hello," said Vinnie, beaming up at Maria.

"Have you come to pay your respects?"

"I have indeed and to give you a belated birthday present," Vinnie said handing Maria his phone. "My top-of-the-range model arrived this morning and I won't be needing this one anymore. I left my old SIM card in and there's still a little credit left so you're good to go."

"You're a darlin'!" Maria replied, giving Vinnie a hug. "My very first iPhone."

She put the phone in her pocket and then she added quickly:

"I'm meeting Helen here when this is over and I'd like you to come along too. Can you hang around for a while?"

Sixty minutes later as the last of the villagers filed outside, Deirdre rose from her seat and lit a cigarette.

"I know, I know, no smoking," she snapped, and she made straight for a group of Mr Browne's friends and relatives who were standing outside.

When the mourners had left, Maria asked her father if Helen and Vinnie could come in for a while.

"Yes they can. I'm going over to the church to see about the arrangements for the funeral tomorrow," he said closing the door behind him.

"What's the story then?" Vinnie asked, and as Maria filled him in about her dream in more detail, his eyes grew wider and wider.

"My dad told me when I was seven I can help dead people. He said it's a gift," Maria said in conclusion.

"That's pretty heavy," Vinnie replied.

"We're not sure exactly what the gift is, but maybe we can find out now," Helen said. "One dead body," she gestured to Mr Browne, "may I present, one dead body communicator," she said pointing at Maria with her other hand. "Let's see what happens when we bring the two of you together."

Maria walked confidently towards the open casket and motioned to her two companions to follow.

Helen scrunched her nose up disapprovingly as she looked down into the casket.

"Ugh! I'm not sure I would choose to display myself in an open coffin when I'm gone, with every man, woman and child in County Kerry peering down at me. Still I suppose with your connections Maria, you could get me a fancy casket with fluffy pillows, a widescreen TV and a big bag of Maltesers?"

"No problemo!" Maria chuckled. "Life as an undertaker's daughter does have its perks."

"I've only ever seen him wear a scruffy football shirt and jeans," said Helen, peering down at Mr Browne.

"His hair has been done and his face made up," Vinnie added. "How come his eyes are shut so tightly?"

"Dad takes care of it in the embalming room," Maria replied, "along with the other gory bits."

"Perhaps you need to have direct contact with the body to make this work," Vinnie suggested, gingerly opening a few buttons on Mr Browne's shirt.

Maria took a deep breath and raised her hands aloft theatrically. She placed them gently onto Mr Browne's midriff.

Nothing could be heard apart from the distant 'meep-meep' of a text message being received.

"I'd better get it," said Vinnie. "Mum will be wondering where I've got to," he said reaching into his pocket. But when he looked at the phone, there was no text message to be seen!

As Vinnie was scratching his head, Helen sighed:

"How disappointing! Maybe we're not doing it right."

"What did you think he would do, sit up and dance?" Vinnie asked, still looking with a puzzled expression at his phone.

"No, but what with the '*HELP ME*', Helen said, mimicking Maria's deep, gravelly voice, "I was expecting a little bit more of a show."

After a few moments, Maria suggested:

"I could try again."

Her two companions nodded in agreement.

"I'll open another shirt button," said Vinnie.

Again Maria held her hands aloft and planted them firmly on Mr Browne's chest.

This time the 'meep-meep' of a text message followed immediately.

"Nothing, nada, zilch, zippo!" said Helen. "I don't understand it. Maybe your powers only work at night or could it be that..."

Helen stopped in her tracks as she saw Maria standing transfixed, a look of surprise on her face.

"What is it?" Helen gasped breathlessly.

"The text message is coming from your old phone, the one you gave me an hour ago," Maria said to Vinnie, taking it out of her pocket.

Maria opened the phone and her face went pale. She turned the phone towards her friends. On screen was an incoming video message. It was from Mr Browne, the dead farmer, lying in the casket in front of them!

End Chapter Three

Chapter Four

The children stared at the phone in disbelief.

"What are we going to do?" Helen asked, her hands trembling with fear.

"We only have one choice," Maria replied, through gritted teeth. "We watch the message."

She beckoned her friends forward and pressed 'play'.

On screen they saw what looked like the inside of a photo booth. A shadowy figure was seated, but the picture was too dark and grainy to make out any of the detail. The seconds continued to tick by without a word being said.

Sixteen, seventeen, eighteen and then, the figure in the video spoke:

"Maria," it growled in such a deep, rasping voice, the hair on the back of her neck leapt to attention. The hoarse voice continued, with a second's space between each word:

"Give... money... in... blue... vase

There was a five second delay before the final words were spoken.

"Must be Anonymous, no name."

A video clip started to play:

It was a promotion for the Tarbert Animal Sanctuary. Owner Maureen Quigley was surrounded by happy, healthy dogs and the children listened intently as Maureen spoke:

"At the Tarbert Animal Sanctuary, rescued dogs are given a home for life where they are treated with respect, compassion and dignity."

As the final word echoed round the room, the video message on Maria's phone vanished.

"Why did you delete it?" Vinnie protested.

"I didn't. It self-destructed, just like in Mission Impossible."

After a few moments Vinnie said:

"The sanctuary is going to close. I read about it in the paper. We got our rescue pup, Bruno from the sanctuary, so the place means a lot to me."

"Did he say vase?" Maria asked.

"Maybe it's one of those Ying or Yang vases. Could be worth a fortune," Helen said, slowly regaining her composure.

"I don't think so," Vinnie replied. "He said money in a vase. It's probably the cash his daughter has been searching for."

"Don't you think we should just tell her?" Helen ventured. "After all she is his only daughter."

"Absolutely not," said Maria. "You didn't see her. She's just wants the loot for herself."

"Besides if we had shown the message we have just seen to a solicitor it would be as good as a last will and testament," Vinnie added. "It's where he wanted his money to go."

"I'd like to make this man's wish come true," Maria announced, turning to face her friends. "Perhaps this is why I have been given this gift, to grant the final wishes of the dead. But I will only do it if we all agree."

Vinnie nodded.

"Bruno would approve," he smiled.

"I can't see what harm there would be making his dream come true," Helen replied, her eyes brightening with excitement. "The daughter sounds like a nasty piece of work. She doesn't deserve the money, so I think it would be great if the animal sanctuary benefitted."

"The problem is going to be getting our hands on the vase. How do we get into the house?" Vinnie added, worry lines appearing on his forehead.

"I've been thinking about it," said Maria. "I have an idea."

* * *

"We thought perhaps you could do with some help," Spencer Lyons said, as the farmhouse door creaked open in the evening sunlight and Deirdre Browne's beady eyes peered out. "I remember what it was like when my wife passed away," he said, still talking through the crack of the door as it remained only slightly ajar. "There were boxes stacked up as far as the eye could see. You'll need to get back to the States so you could probably do with a hand?"

Deirdre Browne bit her lip and pushed the door open a little further so Maria, her two friends and her father could enter.

"To be honest with you, I was going to throw most of it in the skip," Deirdre replied blankly. "But if there's something you can salvage for the charity shop, be my guest."

Maria's eyes were drawn to the mantelpiece, but there was no blue vase to be seen. Any signs of warmth and homeliness in the farmhouse had been stripped away. There were a dozen heavily wrapped boxes in the centre of the room. Black bags were filled to the brim in one corner and an assortment of fresh flowers had been dumped in a small bin.

"I've packed the good stuff ready to be shipped back home," Deirdre said. "But there are some books, bric-a-brac and ornaments I don't want. Anything on the floor in the right hand corner of the room is earmarked for the rubbish dump. Take what you like from it."

There were four boxes of books, ten black plastic bags and three boxes of assorted ornaments in the right hand corner of the room. Spencer Lyons and the children picked up the bags and boxes and carried them out to the car. When they were fully loaded and safely on their way, Maria asked:

"Can we look through the boxes in case there's something we might want?"

"I don't see why not," her father replied. "But you'll have to pay for anything you pick out of your pocket money."

The children excitedly searched through the bags and boxes and minutes later Vinnie held a blue vase aloft.

"Two books and a vase," Spencer Lyons mused as they pulled up outside their house. "The books I understand, but what do you want the vase for?" he said twirling it round in his hand.

"I think it's pretty," Maria replied. "It would look nice in the front of the shop."

Spencer Lyons continued to spin the vase around in his hand and for one horrible moment Maria thought he might drop it. Eventually he said:

"Let's say a euro for the two books and another euro for the vase."

"Done," said Maria.

"What an excellent idea of Maria's to help Deirdre Browne out and you were also thinking of the less well off too," Spencer Lyons said. "I'll drop the rest of the bags down to the charity shop on Monday. I'm sure they will be delighted with our haul."

When they were safely back in her bedroom, Maria reached inside the small blue vase. Right down at the bottom were ten small plastic bank bags, each of them contained twenty €50 notes.

"Wow. There's ten thousand euro in there!" Vinnie exclaimed, calculating quickly. "It could really help a lot of people."

"Remember the money is not ours," Maria cautioned, as she turned to face Vinnie. "Our job is to make Mr Browne's dying wish come true. Are we still agreed?"

Helen and Vinnie nodded.

"Helen you sort out my bike and trainers for tomorrow. Vinnie find a fat envelope for the money and remember what you have to write on the front. It has to be an anonymous donation. Do it in your best hand-writing. We'll go to the animal sanctuary together when everyone else in the village is at the funeral tomorrow."

End Chapter Four

Chapter Five

Every Sunday morning Maria would rise at a quarter past seven. She loved the peace and quiet of the early weekend mornings. After getting dressed, she would slip quietly out the front door and walk. Her favourite spot if the weather was fine was to stroll along the Shannon Estuary. She would take the narrow turn into one of Tarbert's woodland walks, sit underneath a sprawling silver fir tree, close her eyes and think.

The sun peeped in at her this particular Sunday morning to see what was up because Maria stayed twenty minutes longer under the tree than normal.

When Maria got back to her house, she went through her father's long black overcoat which was hanging on the back of the chair and took out the key to his office. While her father was still asleep upstairs, Maria tiptoed up to the door, turned the key in the lock and pushed it open for the very first time.

A damp musty smell filled her nostrils. There was a desk covered with papers and a towering bookcase filled to the brim with unopened volumes. Everything seemed dusty and uncared for. Maria was about to leave when she noticed a small curtain in the corner of the room.

"No more secrets," Maria muttered as she flung open the curtain.

Maria's eyes widened and she dropped the key to the office on the floor with a rattle.

"Angel, my angel," Maria said, holding her hands aloft.

Behind the curtain was a carefully maintained shrine to her mother. The centrepiece of the memorial was an ornate wedding dress with a curved neckline bodice, flanked on either side by framed photographs of Maria's parents on their happy day.

There were bunches of fresh flowers and a book of condolences which Maria flicked open and began to read.

"What the hell are you doing?" Spencer Lyons boomed, shattering the silence. "I told you never to come in here."

His face reddened and he raised his hand as if to slap his daughter, but Maria stood upright and unafraid.

"I wanted to find out about mum," Maria said calmly. "You can hit me if you wish. But I'm old enough to know what happened to her."

Maria's father fell to his knees and started to cry. Maria stood a little distance away, not exactly sure what to do.

"Dad," she whispered softly. "Did she die because of me? Is that the reason you don't love me?"

Her father's sobbing eased slightly.

"Don't you remember the fire?" he asked, wiping away some of the tears.

Maria shook her head.

"I got here just before the fire brigade and rushed upstairs. There were flames everywhere. I picked you up. You begged mum to save your... bear. She smiled, almost as if she knew what was going to happen. She was half way down when the staircase collapsed. I can still see her falling as if it were yesterday."

"Oh my God," Maria said, tears streaming along her eyelids. "She did die because of me."

"No my darling, she didn't," Spencer sobbed, holding his arms open wide to embrace his daughter. "I'm to blame. If only I had made it home two minutes earlier she would have been safe."

For a few moments father and daughter just sat together sobbing in each other's arms. Then Maria said: "But there are no photos of mum anywhere in the house apart from here. I thought you had forgotten about her."

"I'll never forget her. She was the love of my life. There isn't a day I don't wish she was here with me."

"But she is here with you," Maria said softly. "In me."

"Do you remember her singing to you at night?" Spencer asked.

He began to sing:

'If that velvet cloth is coarse,

Mama's going to buy you a rocking horse.'

And then Maria joined in with her father for the next two lines....

'And if that rocking horse won't rock,

Mama's going to buy you a cuckoo clock'.

"Dad, mum's OK. I saw her after she died. She stood at the end of my bed smiling, her eyes were open and she waved at me as she went up through the ceiling. She looked so pretty I thought she was my angel."

"You never told me."

"I didn't think you would believe me," Maria replied. "Besides you might have started camping out in my bedroom, hoping for a second visit."

Spencer laughed softly through the tears.

"Dad we'll never forget mum, but we need to get on with our lives. It was five years ago."

"Five years, one month and twelve days."

Maria handed him a handkerchief and he blew his nose with a strange honking sound.

"Do you remember how one day when you weren't working, we just decided to take the hearse out for a drive?" Spencer asked.

"I do," Maria replied. "I remember how the cars on the road parted like the Red Sea to let us through and the looks we got when we placed our order at the drive-thru in McDonalds."

Spencer laughed and Maria's face darkened for a moment.

"Dad, my dreams have started to come real."

And Maria explained over the next few minutes to her father what had happened. Throughout he sat and listened expressionless until she had finished.

Spencer went over to his desk, opened the bottom drawer and took out a business card which he handed to Maria.

"Your mother brought me to see this man ten years ago. He made me promise to keep this business card somewhere safe for you. He said there would come a time when my daughter would need to contact him and I think the time is now."

Maria peered at the card. It had a photo of an owl peering out of some branches and it said:

'Fester Henry. Clairvoyant. 'Your date with destiny' and at the bottom was a local telephone number.

"The card's a bit naff isn't it," said Maria.

"Well it was ten years ago, but I can tell you this man is excellent. Give him a call," said Spencer, handing Maria the phone.

Maria dialled the number on the card.

After two short rings a croaky voice said:

"Hello Maria. Fester speaking. Meet me on Monday after school at 4pm on the dot. Bring your father. I will be where he met me ten years ago. Oh by the way, you're quite right our business cards are a bit naff. See you on Monday afternoon."

End Chapter Five

Chapter Six

The funeral procession started on Sunday morning at 11 am outside Lyons' removal home in the centre of Tarbert. Maria and her father walked in front, Deirdre Browne and her relatives directly behind. Following the family was the hearse and then the people of the village, on foot and in cars.

Maria and her father walked slowly past the old police station, closed by the Government cutbacks and turned past the statue of the Virgin Mary into the main square. Villagers stood with their heads bowed, hats off, many made the sign of the cross as the hearse drove by and then joined the procession at the back.

The bleak church loomed into view, with its imposing graveyard opposite the bungalow where Maria lived.

Behind her Maria could hear Deirdre Browne moaning:

"I couldn't find any of his money, I don't what the old git did with it," she complained to her aunt. "I've turned the house upside down. It's almost as if it disappeared into thin air," she said and although Maria was pleased, she dared not even muster a flicker of a smile.

The coffin was carried into the dark, unwelcoming church. Maria had always felt uneasy inside and the statue of Padre Pio glared at her angrily from one of the many alcoves.

"Dad I'm feeling a little lightheaded, I'm going to get some air."

Her father nodded as Maria blessed herself, opened the door and stepped outside. She acknowledged the last of the villagers who were hurrying inside and made her way round to the back of the church where Helen and Vinnie were waiting.

"Wow, what a cool bike," Maria said when she saw Helen's shiny new bicycle. "Twenty one gears too, which will take you to the top of any mountain dirt track. Where did you get it?"

"My dad got it for me. It was a lovely surprise. I came downstairs and there it was all wrapped up for me. Dad said presents aren't just for Christmas or birthdays. If you love someone, you can surprise them with a present anytime you like."

"Vinnie, you'll have to buy me a motor bike next year for my birthday with all that money you have sloshing around," Maria said. "A nice blue one with a built in SatNav will do the trick."

"And you can buy me a car," Helen joked. "One of those fancy Audis would be lovely."

"You do think of me as more than just a bank, don't you?" Vinnie frowned.

Maria saw the expression on her friend's face and came straight over to him.

"We're only pulling your leg, it's your friendship not your money we value, you dodo," Maria said, rubbing Vinnie's hair affectionately.

"We would be friends if you were as poor as a church mouse," Helen added and Vinnie smiled, seemingly reassured.

"Maria your trainers are in the bag along with the envelope with the cash," Vinnie said "and your bike is over there against the wall. I saw Maureen from the animal sanctuary go inside the church earlier, so we're clear to go.

"Will there be any security cameras at the sanctuary?" Helen asked.

"Not a chance," Vinnie replied. "Who'd want to break into an animal sanctuary?" he said looking at his watch. "We'd better get going. We need to get there and back before anyone notices."

There was not a villager in sight as the children rode together for a little over five miles before pulling up outside the animal sanctuary.

"Sack the stylist," Helen laughed, pointing at Maria as she climbed off her bike, dressed from head to toe in black, apart from her pair of orange trainers.

Maria stood for a few moments and looked at the sign outside the entrance to the sanctuary – 'we never turn away an animal in need' - before taking the fat envelope from her rucksack. On the front of the envelope Vinnie had written the words: "Anonymous donation to save Tarbert Animal Sanctuary."

The sanctuary was a working farm with ducks, chickens and geese mingling happily with abandoned dogs, cats and horses. As Maria approached the front door, the wind seemed to whip up, as if it were murmuring to her disapprovingly.

"There's no turning back now," Maria said steelily as she popped the envelope inside the letter box.

The return journey was back uphill and the wind was much stronger.

"There's a storm coming," Helen said, and she pointed to dark clouds overhead which were fast approaching.

The children dropped their bikes at Maria's house and arrived back at the church just as the heavens opened and the rain started to teem down. As the coffin was carried out towards the graveyard, Maria's father put his hand on his daughter's shoulder.

"Feeling any better?"

Maria smiled to herself.

"I feel much better, dad. Much, much better."

*   *   *

Vinnie was an only child living in a modern five-bedroom, two-storey house his dad had built on the outskirts of Tarbert. Helen and Maria followed him up the windy spiral staircase to his bedroom.

He picked some books on science and beginner Japanese which were lying on his bedroom floor, put them on his desk and invited Helen and Maria to sit on his sumptuous leather recliner sofa in his bedroom.

"I could get used to this," Helen said, stretching her hands out. "Living in the lap of luxury."

Vinnie snorted.

"Money's not everything it's cracked up to be," he protested. "I would swop my life with either of yours in a heartbeat. The next ten years are planned out for me, down to the very last detail, but I don't get to have a say. What if I want to do something different?"

Maria looked at Helen knowingly.

"Have a look at this," Vinnie said his cheeks reddening as he quickly changed the subject.

He handed Maria an old fashioned radio.

"My Grandma loves listening to this wireless. She got this ancient radio as a wedding present 50 years ago. Since she's come to live with us, she's been slapping, banging or fiddling with it, trying to tune it in properly. It crackles and hisses so badly she asked me to have a look at it. Truth is, it's on its last legs.

So I bought a top of the range digital radio for her and I'm fitting it inside the old wireless casing. The crackling and hissing will be gone forever and when I'm finished she'll never know her fixed up wireless is really a completely new radio."

The two girls smiled in approval and Vinnie took the radio back before asking Maria:

"What do you think will happen tonight in your dream now you've safely delivered the money?"

"Dunno," Maria replied. "Will a voice say 'game over' or will I get a new mission with a new body, I guess we'll just have to wait and see."

"Does everyone who dies in Tarbert end up standing near the wardrobe at the bottom of your bed?"

"No," Maria replied firmly. "I'm guessing some people were happy with their lives and didn't have a dying wish they were burning to have fulfilled. I get a visitor about once a fortnight. John the Postman was the first to open his eyes. I thought it might be a one-off until Mr Browne started speaking."

"Do they try and touch you?" Helen asked a look of repulsion on her face.

"No, they reach out and up, but they are rooted to the spot."

"Have you told your dad the dead are talking to you?" Vinnie asked. "He might be able to give you some explanations."

"I only told him yesterday. Any time I tried before he always seemed so angry."

"Really?" said Vinnie, his eyebrows raised in surprise. "But he seems so calm and friendly to me."

"You're right," Maria remarked. "The only person he's angry with... is me."

"What about if we had a sleepover tonight to see what happens?" Helen asked.

"I don't think it would be safe," Maria replied.

"I see," Vinnie said knowingly.

"I mean it. I can handle it, but you're not used to it yet."

"How do you mean yet?" Helen asked.

"I have a feeling we are only at the beginning of our adventure."

"You have a video recorder on your iPhone," said Vinnie. "It has tons of memory, so it can record continuously for up to four hours. Set it up tonight before you go to bed and then tomorrow we'll be able to see if anything happens. Will you do that at least?"

Maria nodded in agreement.

*   *   *

As Maria lay asleep she saw Mr Browne at the end of the bed near her wardrobe. His eyes were wide open and he held his hands aloft as if he were reaching up to someone. A bright light appeared in the ceiling and Mr Browne beamed with delight as he rose slowly off the ground towards it.

Near the foot of the bed, a black cloud began to form. Dark, gnarly fingers reached out trying to claw Mr Browne back down, but he continued to ascend. It seemed to Maria as if he was protected by an invisible shield and the hands were scraping despairingly at the outside of it. Last to disappear were Mr Browne's twinkly silver boots and then he was gone.

The dark fingers began to whirl furiously and started to form into a shape, all in black apart from a pair of searing red eyes.

"Meddler, dabbler, interferer," said the dark figure, "you know not what you have done!"

End Chapter Six

Chapter Seven

"Who are you?" Maria said bravely.

"I am Laertes, the bridge-builder," the dark figure replied menacingly.

"Well you're not building any bridges here tonight. What do you want?"

"You will desist helping those who have passed," Laertes said testily.

"Will I now?" Maria said, her confidence growing. "It appears I have to face down yet another bully. And where did you learn to speak English, in a cave? '*You will desist from helping those who have passed*'" she said, mimicking Laertes' haunting voice. "Those who have passed what? Passed their exams, passed out, passed go?"

"You are meddling in matters you do not comprehend."

"I comprehend perfectly," Maria said, leaning forward in her bed. "I saw joy written over Mr Browne's face as he rose to what I guess is a better place when we made his last wish come true. And we probably saved hundreds of animals from being destroyed as well."

"You do not comprehend."

"Explain it to me then."

"Hope is built on the ashes of despair."

"You're right, I do not comprehend.

"Watch," Laertes cautioned.

He raised a finger, pointed at Maria's wardrobe and a screen appeared.

"Cool," Maria said. "You can leave the TV here when you go."

A video started to play. It was Maureen Quigley, owner of the animal sanctuary. She was surrounded by canvases and beautiful ink drawings in what looked like an art gallery.

"Animals and drawing are my two passions," Maureen said. "I worked in Ireland at an animal sanctuary and spent my time drawing at night. When the sanctuary closed, due to lack of funding, I came to America. I was constantly drawing and sketching animals, capturing their amazing diversity. One day John Griegg at the Museum of Modern Art in New York saw what I was doing and fell in love with my work. Now I spend my time creating the most wonderfully detailed animal portraits. I miss my friends and family in Ireland, but I am so lucky to be living my dream."

The TV screen disappeared back into the wardrobe.

"Success built on the ashes of failure." Laertes insisted. "This was to be her future but you destroyed it. Do you understand now?"

Maria was silent for a moment.

"I understand perfectly," Maria said finally. "We need to find another way for John Griegg to see Maureen's ink drawings. It would mean she can keep the animal sanctuary open AND get to follow her dream."

"MEDDLER, DABBLER, INTERFERER."

"Yes I think we've been over this before."

"You would dare to meddle yet again?"

"Now you've shown me what needs to be done, absolutely."

"You will DESIST!" said Laertes, shaking the bed so vigorously, Maria's teddy bear Bertrando tumbled to the floor. And for the first time Maria was a little bit frightened.

*   *   *

On Monday morning Maria's father had to come in and wake her from a deep sleep.

"Time for school," her father said softly. "I let you lie in because you were so worn out yesterday. I've packed your lunch and your schoolbag."

Maria was ten minutes late. As she stepped into the classroom, her teacher motioned to her to take her seat.

"As you know this is our last week before our Summer holidays," the teacher said to great applause. "So this morning as a treat we'll be watching a DVD called School of Rock and we'll have a discussion about it afterwards. Then this afternoon I've invited Maureen Quigley from the Tarbert Animal Sanctuary to come in and talk to us."

Maria's eyebrows raised and Helen and Vinnie looked at each other in surprise.

"She'll be telling us about the different animals she looks after. And perhaps because the animal sanctuary is under threat of closure, you might know of a loving home for some of them?" Ms Kearns suggested.

"I know what to do with them miss," Mark sniggered from the back of the class.

Maria turned around and glared at him.

"Have you something to add Mark?" the teacher asked encouragingly.

Mark looked at Ms Kearns and then back at Maria again.

"I could ask my mum if we could let one of the animals stay with us miss," he said meekly.

And as the teacher applauded Mark's selflessness, Maria smiled knowingly to herself.

*   *   *

"Maureen Quigley coming in, it seems like a bit of a coincidence," Vinnie said to Maria at lunchtime.

"I don't believe in coincidences," Maria replied sternly.

"What went on last night," Helen said, coming over to join them and Maria filled them both in.

"The big news was the dark visitor," Maria concluded. "He called himself Laertes."

"Let come what comes; only I'll be revenged. Most thoroughly for my father I dare damnation," Vinnie said, standing up theatrically.

Both the girls applauded and Vinnie bowed.

"Tell us more?" Maria encouraged.

"That was Laertes, he's the guy who kills Hamlet in the play by William Shakespeare," Vinnie continued. "Would you like to hear some more?"

"Did you have the video recorder on?" Helen said, ignoring Vinnie's pleas for extra stage time. "We might get to see what Laertes looked like."

"I never checked it," Maria said fumbling in her pocket and holding her phone up to the light. "It's recorded all right. I have one massive file in there."

"I'll have a look at it," said Vinnie and he started to scroll adeptly through the video.

After a few moments Vinnie said:

"You are fast asleep right the way through the video. There's no figure rising at the end of the bed and no sign of Laertes. It looks like it's all going on in your head," said Vinnie.

He was about to hand the phone back to Maria when he suddenly he went "Whoa".

"Look at this," Vinnie said and the two girls huddled round the phone as he played a section towards the end of the video.

"Your bed is definitely moving and your bear just seemed to leap off it to freedom," Vinnie said.

Maria explained how Laertes had insisted she stop communicating with the dead and had got enraged when she had refused to do so.

"What are you going to do?" Vinnie and Helen asked in unison.

"We're going to continue," Maria replied sternly. "This power was given to me and I will not let bullies on earth or from the other side rule my life for me."

*   *   *

"You are one of the first to know," a beaming Maureen Quigley, owner of Tarbert Animal Sanctuary said, as she addressed the children after lunch. "A little miracle has happened and the animal sanctuary will remain open."

The children applauded and cheered.

"I had a very generous anonymous donation which will allow us to keep going. I have a photo shoot with the Kerryman newspaper and the Kerry's Eye today so I feel like a rock star! It will make such a difference to the animals and their welfare."

"Laertes won't be pleased," Vinnie whispered.

Maureen had brought five animals in for the children to see and play with and she had also brought in ink drawings of each of the animals.

"Those are magnificent," said Ms Kearns. "I used to work with a man in the Museum of Modern Art in New York called John Griegg. He would love these. Would you mind if I took a photo of them on my camera-phone and sent them to him?"

"Be my guest," Maureen beamed delightedly and moments later the photos were on their way to New York.

End Chapter Seven

Chapter Eight

"I never knew we had a clairvoyant in Tarbert. Where is he based?" Maria asked her father as they set off together after school.

"Beside the Ferry House."

"Where exactly beside the Ferry House?" quizzed Maria as they turned into the Square.

"Through the yellow door beside the Ferry House. Look, I know it sounds strange, but you'll see when we get there."

Spencer walked with his daughter to the side of the Ferry House and knocked three times at the big yellow door.

The door opened into a courtyard and revealed a flight of steps leading down to a basement which they carefully descended.

"Come in, come in," said a white-haired man with a pair of glasses perched on the end of his nose. He was wearing an apron which said 'Kentucky Fried Chicken' on the front. "And you must be Maria. I am Fester. Please take a seat."

Fester's desk was piled high with paper files. There were so many papers, when he sat down, he was unable to see Maria and her father over the top of them. He moved some of them to one side.

"Ahhh, much better. We don't often get guests down here. We only invite the real VIPs you know. Your parents were here ten years ago and now you. Would you like some coffee?"

"No thanks," Maria replied. "You don't look much like a clairvoyant," Maria said. "Aren't you supposed to have long earrings and a crystal ball instead of a Kentucky Fried Chicken apron?"

"We do things a little differently here when predicting the future. We have a file on you and a file on lots of other people. We have lots and lots of files. Lester would you bring me Maria Lyons' file PLEASE," Fester shouted.

"No problem," called a voice from somewhere in the basement.

"Most of our work is done by messengers," Fester said, adjusting his thin spectacles. "Let's say your destiny is to manage a cinema. You might bump into someone who tells you about a job there. Coincidence? Unlikely. Often we given that person the very piece of information necessary to let you fulfil your true destiny."

Lester continued to rummage noisily through filing cabinets in the distance.

"Like today with Ms Quigley and her ink drawings?" Maria asked. "Was it your handiwork getting her discovered by John Griegg in New York?"

"How very perceptive of you," Fester marvelled. "We usually work in ways which are more subtle, but it came through as a rush job," he said scratching his chin. "You see we prefer to take time to meet VIPs or catalysts as we call them like yourself and help to put them on the right path. It's not about good and evil, right or wrong. We're not on your side or against you. It's just about change management. Even chaos needs to be managed."

Fester took a slurp out of his coffee and winced.

"Cold," he said. "I wonder how long it's been there."

He shook his head.

"As for the apron, we also operate the franchise to sell Kentucky Fried Chicken here in Tarbert. It's finger lickin' good! We've been open for ten weeks now and it's going really well. I'm surprised you haven't paid us a visit."

Maria looked blankly at Fester.

"But we don't have a Kentucky Fried Chicken shop in Tarbert."

"Found it," said Lester

Maria turned to see another old man surface from behind two huge stacks of paper. His resemblance to Fester was uncanny. The only difference Maria could see between them was Fester's glasses were blue and Lester's were green.

"Your brother?" Maria asked.

"In this job with so many files, it helps to come from a big family," Fester replied. "Now let me see what we have here. Ah yes," he continued, "you are indeed a very special child. Your most likely destiny is," he said, turning to the last page, "to become one of the six."

He slammed the file shut triumphantly.

"What are the six?"

"You haven't told her anything?" Fester gestured to Spencer.

Maria's dad shook his head.

"You've been having dreams with dead people wiggling their fingers at you, right?" Fester said.

Maria nodded.

"Every child has a different task. In your case, you'll know by now you can make the last wish of the dead come true?"

"I've already made one come true."

"Good for you. We think there are about ten children who have this special power. What you need to do to become one of the six is to make three dying wishes come true within 30 days of your 12th birthday. When were you twelve?"

"Ten days ago."

"So you've two wishes to go and twenty days to do them in, simple as that. But there is no guarantee – at the moment, becoming one of the six is just your most likely destiny."

"How imprecise your language is for a clairvoyant! It seems like guesswork. Don't you know what will happen to me?"

"No. We operate on a system of best estimates. But with the information we have at our fingertips," he said gesturing to the mountain of files, "our best guesses are usually pretty accurate. Although it may be your destiny to be one of the six, there are forces out there who would prefer you didn't. Do not mock what you do not understand."

"Why does everyone speak in such mysterious ways," Maria sighed. "You sound just like Laertes."

Fester's face went white. He rushed forward and held Maria tightly.

"What do you know of Laertes," he hissed.

"Nothing, he just came to me in my dreams."

"You've met? He rarely appears in person. Laertes wants an orderly future, but despite what he says to you, it's not the way things are meant to be. Blips, anomalies, call them what you like, the uncertainties and unpredictability of the universe, rather than the files we have here make life exciting! How long have you being having the dreams?"

"Since I was seven."

"It suggests the power is strong within you."

"And what happens if I don't make three wishes come true?"

"If you have not fulfilled the third wish within thirty days of your twelfth birthday, your powers will disappear and your dreams will return to normal. But if you become one of the six you will continue to have the power until your 18th birthday. Now I need to speak to your father for one minute. Please wait upstairs. He will be with you in sixty seconds precisely."

Maria climbed the stairs into the open air. Sitting on a bench was a man who looked exactly like Fester, but his glasses were purple.

"Lester?" Maria asked.

"No, I'm Chester," the man chuckled. "There are a few of us working down there."

"I have been past this way many times before and never noticed this basement."

"Are you sure? You must be mistaken," said Chester, opening a box of Kentucky Fried Chicken. "We have always been here."

Chester offered Maria a piece of chicken and she took one.

"What do you think Fester is telling my dad?" she said biting into the chicken.

"Many people close doors which should be left open. I'm guessing your father is being told to leave as many doors open as possible. But I'm only 98 per cent certain," Chester smiled.

"This is delicious," Maria said. "Can I get a piece for my dad?"

"No problem. If you want more, we're up the road next to Swanky's Bar," said Chester going back in.

Moments later Maria's father emerged looking thoughtful. He put his arm round his daughter.

"Piece of chicken for you?" Maria said handing it to her dad and they munched their way home.

When she went to bed later that evening, no late-night visitors gathered at the bottom of her bed and for the first time in years, Maria had a great night's sleep.

End Chapter Eight

Chapter Nine

Maria sat with her charcoals in the kitchen, drawing. In the foreground she had sketched out Laertes with his searing eyes and shock of blonde, spiked hair. In the background of the picture she drew a large imposing house with many windows surrounded by trees. The shades were drawn so they were exactly the same in each room.

Where had her mother gone, Maria thought as she drew? Was it to be processed by someone like Laertes? Her mother was such a delicate flower. It repulsed her to think of Laertes shoving her mother on a conveyor belt somewhere on the other side. And yet the look on Paul Browne's face when he ascended through the ceiling had filled her with hope."

"Your friends are here," Spencer said.

Vinnie and Helen trooped into the kitchen. After Spencer closed the door behind them, Vinnie shook his head vigorously.

"It's been ten days. Ten long boring, empty days. And we've had nothing. Not a sausage, not a whimper."

"Maria can't help it," Helen said indignantly, as she finished off a currant bun. "What do you want her to do? Pray for people to hurry up and die?"

Vinnie looked over and saw Maria's cheeks redden slightly.

"Something's happened, hasn't it?" he said eagerly.

"Dad's been in the embalming room all afternoon," Maria replied, with a gleam in her eye. "When someone dies, he normally works right through until 6," she said looking up at the clock as it tiptoed past 5.50. "We'll wait until dad goes across to the church to make the arrangements. Then we can slip inside to see if our visitor has a dying wish."

"Do you know who it is?" Helen asked.

"Betty O' Leary," Maria replied.

"Romantic Ireland's dead and gone," Vinnie said theatrically.

Helen and Maria both glared at Vinnie.

"It's with O'Leary in the grave," he said with a flourish. "Stick with me and I'll educate you both yet. It's a poem by W B Yeats."

"Was she the old lady who lived with her brother Cormac up on the hill?" Helen asked ignoring Vinnie's antics.

"She wasn't very old, 60 I think," Maria replied. "Her brother's very upset about it. She died in her sleep early this morning."

"Don't the horse-face sisters live with the O' Leary's?" Vinnie asked, changing the subject.

"They live in the flat upstairs," Maria said. "Although I don't think the girls would appreciate your nickname for them. Haven't you heard about beauty being skin deep?"

"Yes I have," said Vinnie. "But those girls are nasty to go with it. I saw the two of them in town shopping with Cormac last week. It looked like they had him wrapped round their little fingers."

"Rhonda is as hard as nails with a voice which can break glass," Maria said. "The only person worse than her is Wanda her sister."

"Wanda and Rhonda?" Helen exclaimed. "You've got to be kidding. How come I've never met this pair?"

"You don't know how lucky you are," Vinnie replied. "They moved over from Limerick about three weeks ago. If we were putting Cinderella on in the town hall, the horse face sisters would get two of the parts for sure."

Maria put her finger to her lips and moments later the children heard Spencer Lyons close the front door behind him and start to walk across the road towards the church.

"Now's our chance," said Maria and she motioned to her friends to follow her.

The door to the embalming room creaked opened. Lying on the slab in front of the children was Betty O'Leary, with her hair done and face made up.

"She looks like a doll," said Vinnie. "How come she looks so good?"

"It's all part of the service. They come out from the embalming room spruced up and manicured," Maria replied. "First my dad stitches their eyeballs shut, seals up the mouth and drains the bodily fluids. Men *and* women are shaved to get rid of any hairy bits. The make-up is applied to give the lips some colour and Mrs Hourigan comes in to style their hair. It's hilarious. I hear her chatting away to the dead bodies as she's doing it – 'how are you today?' or 'what are we having done this morning?'

Helen laughed and Maria leaned forward excitedly.

"Sometimes when Mrs Hourigan is blow drying she starts singing. Often they are not the most appropriate songs in the world. I was in stitches the other day when she was belting out this song by the Bee Gees."

Maria threw her hands out overdramatically and started singing:

'Ah, ha, ha, ha, stayin' alive, stayin' alive'.

She beckoned to her two friends to join in and the three of them sang the last line of the chorus in fits of giggles:

'Ah, ha, ha, ha, stayin' alive.'

"Helen would you mind giving me a hand?" Maria asked after they had stopped laughing and Helen opened a couple of buttons of Betty O' Leary's blouse.

"Here goes nothing," Maria said, raising her hands in the air and laying them to rest on Betty's chest.

The 'meep-meep' of the text came almost immediately and the children huddled nervously around Maria's phone as she pressed play.

Staring out at them was a figure sitting in the same grainy photo booth.

It seemed like an eternity, but it was only twenty seconds until the shadow spoke.

"Maria..... stop..them," it said chillingly.

A video clip began. It was the inside of Swanky's Bar and restaurant in Tarbert. The video zoomed in on a table where Cormac, Betty's brother was seated with Rhonda, one of the 'horse-faced' sisters.

"She's the small, hairy one, not the large, smelly one," said Vinnie. "From a distance she's slightly better looking."

"Sshh," Helen insisted.

In the video clip, Cormac reached into his pocket, took out a small box and placed it in front of Rhonda.

"This ring has been in my family for generations," said Cormac. "Will you marry me?"

"Of course I will," Rhonda replied blankly, getting up to leave the table. "Just let me ring my sister and tell her the news."

"The sap has proposed," Rhonda said when she was safely out of earshot. "It's a mouldy old ring but who cares. Three months from now the farmhouse and twenty acres of prime pastureland will be mine."

As the final word echoed round the room, the video message on Maria's phone vanished.

"Before you ask," Maria said. "It deleted itself again."

"Shame," said Vinnie. "We could have used it to show Cormac. Love can make some people blind," said Vinnie.

"It can make some people stay together when they should really separate," said Maria.

Helen shifted uneasily in her seat.

"What do you mean?"

"I mean he obviously loves her but she just loves his land, so they are not a perfect match."

"I see," said Helen testily. "I thought you were talking about someone else.

"I have an idea," said Vinnie. "We need a volunteer to ask Rhonda three simple questions. But the sisters know me, so they won't trust me," said Vinnie.

"They've met me too," said Maria, as they both turned to look at Helen.

"Oh no, no way," said Helen. "Whatever plan you have in mind you can leave me out of it."

"You'll be as safe as houses," Vinnie insisted. "We'll hook you up with a hidden camera so you can capture the answers and we'll give you an earpiece so we can communicate with you too. If they confess, we can show the footage to Cormac afterwards. We'll be with you every step of the way."

"So I'm just going to waltz up to her, ask her three questions and she's going to reveal everything? This is your grand plan?"

"That's about it."

"It's feeble," said Helen.

"Do you have a better one?" Vinnie asked.

****

Three hours later Vinnie had prepared the script for the telephone call. He was using computer software to make his voice sound deeper.

"Hello am I speaking to Rhonda?" said Vinnie in a voice so deep, the two girls giggled with delight.

"Yes," came the curt reply. "But I don't need insurance or double glazing," Rhonda barked.

"We're not trying to sell you anything," Vinnie continued in his extra deep voice. "We have chosen three couples in Kerry who recently got engaged. One lucky couple will win €50,000 to spend on their wedding. All you need to do is answer three simple questions. Are you interested?"

"Not half."

"We'll send our work placement student Helen round tomorrow to your house. Shall we say 4pm?"

End Chapter Nine

Chapter Ten

"C'mon in," said a petite Rhonda opening the front door and Helen stepped inside. For a moment Helen stopped transfixed, staring at Rhonda's small but perfectly groomed moustache, which curled up neatly at the edges.

"Oh my God, look at the Ronnie," said Vinnie through the earpiece and even though Helen wanted to smile, she managed to keep a straight face.

"I see you gawking at my moustache," said Rhonda, stroking her upper lip. "Waxing, threading, creams, I've tried them all but none of them got rid of it permanently. And then I thought to myself, why fight nature? So I grew a full moustache for Movemeber for charity and I've kept it ever since. It's quite trendy, don't you think?"

Everywhere Helen looked there were empty cola bottles and pizza cartons, crisp bags and sweet wrappers. A large flat screen TV was on in the corner of the room and another was mounted in the kitchenette which adjoined the living room.

"It's so we never miss a moment of our favourite programmes," said Wanda, who wobbled out of the kitchen munching a large bag of tortillas. "Would you like a biscuit?" she asked Helen.

As she extended her hand, Helen caught a strong smell of body odour and her face wrinkled in disgust.

"No thanks."

"Good," she chuckled. "There aren't any left."

Rhonda motioned to Helen to sit down.

"I need you to answer three questions for me," Helen said opening her folder and clicking her pen. "Firstly, how did the two of you meet?"

"I met him at the Tarbert dating agency. He was sitting alone in the corridor filling in his form with his gold fountain pen. I noticed like me, he enjoyed bird watching and French film. Imagine my surprise and delight when we got matched for a date."

"Of course, we were as surprised as you Pinocchio," Wanda said choking with laughter, before opening another bag of tortillas.

"Excellent answer," Helen said encouragingly, ignoring Wanda's taunts.

"Two questions left. Was the proposal of marriage romantic?"

"Oh very much so, we went out to dinner and the sap produced a ring from his pocket and got down on one knee to propose."

Helen stopped writing.

"The sap?"

"It's my pet name for him but there's no need to write it down," Rhonda said quickly. "We danced and drank champagne until sunrise. And as for the ring, it's a lovely piece of antique jewellery."

"A mouldy old ring was what you called it," Wanda chipped in.

"Finally what do you think the most important reason is for getting married?" Helen asked.

"True love. If you feel passion in your heart for someone, then it's your destiny to be together."

"Excellent," said Helen writing down the final answer and putting them in an envelope, which she sealed.

"Tell her the truth," Wanda insisted, removing a tortilla chip which had got wedged in her belly button. "I don't know how you managed to answer those questions with a straight face. Every word you spoke was a lie."

"Shush," Rhonda urged.

"The answers remain in the sealed envelope and the judges decide who wins based on what I've written down. So you can tell me anything you want to now, if you wish," Helen said excitedly. She adjusted the pinhole camera so it was pointing squarely at Rhonda.

"One day someone will ask even a plain, unattractive girl like you to marry them," Rhonda said. "Take my advice. Marry someone rich."

"What about love?" Helen interjected.

"Love is important too," Rhonda said, nodding in agreement. "There's no doubt Cormac loves me and the man I love, Richard, is working just five miles away, so I will get the best of both worlds. Cormac's a farmer so he's out in the field during the day. He'll buy me a car so I can pop to the shops and spend, spend, spend. I'll see Richard afterwards and then be back in time for dinner with Cormac. It's my idea of wedded bliss."

Rhonda moved closer to Helen and stared straight into the video camera.

"Even if you were to show him a video, like the one you are recording right now, it wouldn't change his mind."

"Get out of there, you've been rumbled," Vinnie urged Helen through the earpiece.

"What are you talking about," Helen protested, standing up and backing slowly towards the door.

"Don't you know what I do? I work for an electronics shop in Limerick. I know what you have there. A pinhole camera. We sell them to creeps like you who want to snoop on other people," Rhonda snarled.

"Do you think we're dumb?" Wanda added. "I've seen you before. You hang round with morbid Maria and that Vinnie idiot. Work placement my bum."

"And filming this won't do you any good," Rhonda said, as Helen continued to edge towards the door. "You can show the video to Cormac till his cows come home. Cormac if you are listening, I don't love you. I've never told you I love and I never will love you, but I'm going to marry you anyway. I want your land and your house and in return you can live with me, separate rooms, but you know this already."

"The hoity-toity, full of herself librarian even took a shine to your Cormac," Wanda said, putting her arm round her sister. As she did so, there was a squelching sound and Rhonda's nosed curled up.

"She even sent him a poem would you believe, the cheek of her. But we steam open your letters, bet you didn't know that, Cormac! It's for your own good, so we made sure her words hit the trashcan," said Wanda, staring straight into the lens of the camera.

"Now clear off before I lose my temper," Rhonda said shooing Helen out the door.

"Take Cormac's mail before you leave," Vinnie urged as the door slammed behind Helen. "It might be nice for him to read one of his letters in private for a change."

And a shaken Helen picked up a single letter for Conor which was sitting on the doormat downstairs.

End Chapter Ten

Chapter Eleven

"How do you persuade a man who loves the wrong woman to see the light?" Maria asked when the three of them were seated safely in the comfort of Maria's living room.

"If *he's* not going to change then you need to change *her,*" Vinnie replied.

He opened the letter for Conor Helen had brought back from the house."

"I see," Helen said sarcastically. "Thank you for your analysis Dr Freud. Are we really supposed to interfere in people's love lives? And weren't you supposed to be giving the letter to Cormac instead of opening it up like the terrible twins?"

"Hmm," said Vinnie studying the letter. "It's a fundraising request from Lepra, the leprosy charity. It might prove to be useful. So are we agreed we should intervene now we've seen the evidence that she loves someone else?"

"I don't see what it's got to do with us," Helen replied. "Besides in time, maybe she will love him," Helen replied. "The last wish was about money, this is playing with people's emotions. Do you really think it's something we should be doing?"

"I think I've been given this power to help people when they are about to make poor decisions," Maria said firmly. "We know Mary loved her brother very much. I'm not sure the two sisters love anything apart from themselves and Cormac's money. So I think we are absolutely right to help. But we must all be in agreement if we are to proceed. Are we agreed?"

Vinnie first and then Helen nodded.

"But we shouldn't leave Cormac without a partner," Helen said. "I guess the reason he's with Rhonda is she pays him some small bit of attention."

"I've been in his house," Vinnie said. "He has a study filled to the brim with the modern classics and out the back he's got some baby birds. It's his real passion. Leave it to me, I'll build it into my plan."

"Your plan?" said Helen.

"Yes, my plan."

"Would it be anything like your last plan where I ask Rhonda three simple questions?"

"My new improved plan," said Vinnie. "Now I must go and print up some stationery and return my library book."

****

"Laertes won't be pleased with you," Helen said as Maria took the corned beef brisket out from the slow cooker.

"I guess not," Maria replied.

She let the corned beef rest on the counter.

"It smells fantastic," Helen said. "I see you used some apple, what else have you got in there?"

"Just some caraway seeds, a few spices and a little beer," said Maria. "Serve it up with cabbage and potatoes and you're good to go."

"I wish you could come and cook in our house," Helen said, her face darkening. "For dinner we get frozen pizza, frozen chips and frozen burgers."

"Dad will be here in a minute," said Maria, handing Helen her coat. "I know creepy Laertes is telling me not to make these wishes come true but I think we should. You should have seen the smile on Paul Browne's face when he went through my ceiling. It proves we are right to help."

****

Maria closed her eyes hoping for a good night's sleep, but it was not meant to be. Betty O' Leary stood at the end of her bed, her hands held out towards Maria, a blue light coming from her eyes.

"Help me," Mary O' Leary urged softly. "Help me!"

Near the foot of the bed, a dark cloud began to whirl furiously. It started to form into a shape, all in black apart from a pair of searing red eyes. It was Laertes.

"Cease your begging fool," he said, speaking to Betty O' Leary. "You couldn't help yourself when you were down here and she will not help you either."

Laertes pointed at the curtains in Maria's bedroom. They flew off the wall and covered Betty O' Leary from head to foot and Laertes turned his attention to Maria.

"I cannot stand to look at their whiny faces and begging eyes. But you! You are still interfering with the timeline despite my warnings. You do not know the harm you are causing. I will not allow it."

"What's the big deal?" Maria asked casually.

"Change one detail and events which are meant to happen, will not happen. You cannot meddle. You will not meddle! There is an order and a reason beyond your intelligence."

"Tell me what would be so bad if Rhonda didn't marry Cormac? She doesn't love him."

"I shall not explain these things to you, a mere mortal. But what would happen would be even worse than the future you seek to prevent."

"You're lying," said Maria. "What could be worse than marrying Rhonda?"

Laertes eyes flashed a darker kind of red.

"Watch," Laertes cautioned. He raised a finger and the top of it lit up like a candle. He pointed at Maria's wardrobe and the screen appeared once again.

On screen was a video clip of Cormac dressed in a smart suit. He was waiting at the top of the church as his bride walked towards him. Her dress seemed to be a little larger than normal and her face was covered by a veil. She seemed to be putting something into her mouth as she walked up the aisle.

As she reached the top of the church, Cormac smiled. There seemed to be a large crunching noise coming from under the veil as Cormac reached forward to lift it.

"My beautiful bride," Cormac said smiling. "Finish your tortillas and as soon as you are ready, we'll get married."

The video zoomed in. Maria saw for the first time Cormac wasn't marrying Rhonda, but her sister Wanda instead!

"Ugh gross" said Maria. "Snacks at the altar and she's got a sour cream dip too. I see what you mean Laertes. It looks like we need to take both of the sisters out of the picture."

"You would dare proceed after what I have shown you?"

"I'm afraid we have to preserve Cormac's state of mind," Maria said simply. "And in the interests of good taste, we must intervene."

Laertes flew into a rage and shook the bed so hard it started to spin around the bedroom.

"Whee!" said Maria trying to appear brave, but she didn't feel very brave.

"Desist from meddling, dabbler or I will intervene directly. You have been warned."

The curtains tumbled to the floor and Laertes disassembled into a black cloud and disappeared.

End Chapter Eleven

Chapter Twelve

Early the next morning Maria's father came in to her bedroom with some tea and jammy toast for her last day at school before the Summer holidays but she was already washed and fully dressed and sitting on her bed.

"I like the bed in the centre of the room look, but I'm not sure you are using the curtains to their full effect," said Spencer, after he had stopped staring in disbelief at the bedroom's new look.

"I fancied a change Dad," said Maria wolfing down the toast as her father surveyed the damage. "I had a visit from my interior decorator Laertes last night. I think he's a little bit rusty."

"You seem very calm about it. Are you sure you're OK?"

"It'll only be like this for two more wishes and then he'll be gone," Maria replied, crossing her fingers.

"What wish are you working on today?"

"It's a wish of the heart," said Maria grabbing her schoolbag and heading for the front door, "the very best wishes to grant."

Later that day at school Maria explained what had happened to Helen. Vinnie was listening in from the desk behind but he was busily writing something on some fancy headed paper.

"He's been asking me to spell certain words. Me! He knows I can't spell for toffee," said Helen.

Vinnie started folding up the letter neatly. He sealed it inside an envelope, carefully took a used stamp from his pocket and glued it onto the front of the envelope.

"That's not going to fool the post office," Helen protested.

"It's not intended to," said Maria. "Brian the postman owes us a favour. We gave him an extra fancy casket and all the trimmings for no extra charge when his mum passed away so I'm going to ask him to deliver Vinnie's letter by hand.

Maria paused.

"Helen I need you to do something for me," she continued. "I need you to persuade the librarian to have her lunch in the park tomorrow opposite Cormac's house. Vinnie make sure you get Cormac back to his house at 1 pm?"

Vinnie nodded.

"What will I tell the librarian?" Helen pleaded. "What if it's raining? What if she has a meeting? What if she doesn't eat lunch?"

"Tell her exactly what I'll be telling Cormac," Vinnie said. "This is the one chance they have to meet the partner of their dreams."

*****

The following day at ten to one the postman rang the doorbell of the horse-faced sisters flat and Rhonda came down to answer the door.

"Here's your mail and I've got an urgent letter for Cormac too," said the postman. "Would you mind giving it to him?"

"No problem," said Rhonda.

With the door safely closed, the postman gave the thumbs up to Maria.

Ten minutes later Cormac pulled his car up outside his house and Vinnie came over to greet him.

"Now may I suggest you go in and change," Vinnie urged. "Have a shave and put on some fresh clothes. Remember you are getting ready to meet the woman of your dreams."

"I'm only going along with this because I'm guessing it's a romantic lunch arranged with my fiancée, the beautiful Rhonda," Cormac insisted.

Vinnie made a face.

"We're engaged and getting married next year," Cormac said, stepping out of the car and walking up the driveway to his house. As he put his key in the door, he was nearly flattened by the horse-faced sisters bolting out the door, their hands stuffed with suitcases and black plastic bags.

"Rhonda, what's wrong darling?" Cormac asked.

"I knew you were too good to be true. Stay away from me you diseased creature."

"What's the matter?" Cormac protested. "Tell me!"

"Don't pretend to us. We've read your letter from the hospital," said Wanda throwing it at him. "We'll send someone round later for the rest of our stuff."

"And here's your Halloween ring," Rhonda said, tossing Cormac's engagement ring on the floor. "Give it back to your dead granny, I don't want it."

A bewildered Cormac held the letter in his hands as the horse-face sisters bolted past him, loaded up their car and sped off.

"What just happened?" Cormac said, still clutching the letter, tears falling from his eyes.

"I know it's a shock," Vinnie suggested softly. "Why don't you sit in the park and read the letter and see what's it about?"

*****

Cormac had been sitting on a park bench for five minutes when the librarian approached with her lunch.

"What's wrong?" she asked, seeing Cormac's downcast appearance.

"You shouldn't talk to me," Cormac said. "I have a contagious disease, leprosy. It's a bit of a shock though. I didn't even realise I was sick."

"May I read it?" Sandra asked sitting down beside him.

After a few moments the librarian said:

"I think I have some good news for you."

Cormac perked up.

"I don't think this letter is real."

"Why not?"

"Three reasons. Firstly the spelling is awful. For example, there's no 'j' in contagious."

"Well it might just be a mistake."

"True," the librarian nodded. "But the second reason is the name of the doctor who signed the letter. It's signed by Dr Avin Alaff, do you get it? Having a laugh?"

Cormac smiled briefly, but then his face darkened again.

"He could be from Far East," Cormac said. "There are many unusual names out there."

"Once again you may be right," admitted Sandra. "But I have a third and compelling reason. Leprosy is not contagious."

"You're kidding," said Cormac.

"I'm not," Sandra replied. "I did some work with Lepra, the leprosy charity, so I know. You can only catch the disease if you get repeated nose or mouth droplets from someone who has it," she said, taking out some bread to feed the birds.

Cormac had perked up considerably.

"You know I keep some baby birds," said Cormac, who had perked up considerably. "You must come over and see them sometime, if you don't mind visiting someone with leprosy."

"I'd love to," beamed the librarian and the two of them continued to talk together long into the afternoon.

End Chapter Twelve

Chapter Thirteen

As Maria lay asleep she saw Betty O' Leary at the end of her bed near the wardrobe. Her eyes were wide open and she held her hands aloft as if she were reaching up to someone. A bright light appeared in the ceiling and Betty O' Leary beamed with delight as she rose slowly off the ground towards it.

Near the foot of the bed, a dark cloud began to form and black, gnarly fingers reached out trying to claw her back down, but she continued to ascend and moments later she was gone.

The fingers began to whirl furiously and started to form into a shape, all in black apart from a pair of searing red eyes.

"Meddler, dabbler, interferer," said Laertes, "Have you not learned by unfurling one bit of time, you create chaos? I will not have another child defy me in this way. It is time to stop your meddling. I take the Oath of Namartis!"

As soon as the words were spoken, Laertes disassembled into a black cloud and disappeared.

*****

Maria found the church in Tarbert to be extra creepy. Perhaps it was because it was the first gloomy figure on her horizon every morning she opened her curtains or maybe it was something more real. Were probing eyes watching her through the many church peepholes?

She stood in the half darkness in the church at dawn mass as the priest announced from the pulpit: 'first reading'. Maria rose from her seat and nodded to Helen, who was sitting near the front of the church. She walked past the accusatory finger of Brendan the navigator, a sinister looking statue beside the altar and climbed up on to the pulpit.

As Maria read her eyes were drawn to two men sitting in the second row who she had never seen before. They looked identical.

Both were albino, both had clear blue eyes, the same deep blue eyes of the sea which had blinked out at her from Laertes the night before. Was it a coincidence, Maria thought as she stared out at the thinly scattered bleary-eyed congregation? She shook her head, finished the reading and returned to her seat.

As the mass came to an end, Maria noticed the two men were the first to leave the church. Outside Helen came to talk to Maria. Maria couldn't help but notice the bruise underneath Helen's eye.

"Can you meet me at the grotto today at three?" Maria asked.

"No problem," Helen said. "Why the grotto?"

"I can't tell you right now," Maria replied.

"More mysteries," said Helen, sighing heavily. "I guess you're good at secrets."

"I'm not the only one," Maria muttered under her breath.

"What did you say?"

"Nothing, forget I said anything."

"No come on, you have something on your mind, spit it out."

"Well it's just we all have secrets," said Maria.

"Not me," Helen replied. "I'm an open book."

"So where did you get the bruise, the one above your right eye?"

"I'm told you, I'm just clumsy," Helen said indignantly.

"And last week you had a lot of lipstick on because you had a cold sore but it looked to me like someone had hit you in the mouth."

Helen remained quiet.

"And then there was the time you were wearing the short polka-dot skirt, when I saw the bruises on your legs?"

"What are you suggesting?" Helen said angrily, fighting back the tears.

"He hits you, your father, doesn't he? And then he buys you stuff afterwards to make up for it, like your new bike."

"You can forget three pm at the grotto, you're on your own" Helen said, her face crimson red and she stormed out of the church grounds.

****

Later that morning Vinnie popped into the funeral home.

"So glad you dropped by," said Maria. "Will you meet me at three this afternoon outside the grotto in the square? Don't be late."

"Sure. Is Helen coming too?"

"No. We had a fight. I asked her about her bruises."

"Oh brother," Vinnie said.

"You know he hits her," Maria replied. "That's our friend getting slapped around, but she loves her dad, so she never says a bad word about him."

"How did she react?"

"She didn't say much, but her face looked like thunder."

"I think you should apologise."

"But why? I'm her best friend. If she doesn't face up to it, it's never going to stop."

"But it's something she needs to do herself, I don't think it's up to us to intervene."

"We know her father comes home late at night sometimes having spent all day in the pub. It's not right, it's just not right."

"I think you should apologise," Vinnie said. "He seems like a good man to me."

"Thank you. Advice noted. Nobody is a good man if they hit their children. Now tell me, will you be there at 3pm this afternoon?"

"I'll be there."

"Thank you, I'm depending on you."

****

Maria's words kept ringing in Vinnie's ears as he ran down the street.

"I'll meet you at the grotto in the square at three, don't be late."

If I keep running, he told himself, I'll make it.

As he turned round the penultimate corner, Vinnie could see the emergency lights of a police car whirring which had cordoned off the square. He pushed through the line of villagers where a brightly coloured tape was stretched across the road – 'police – do not cross'. Standing on the other side of the tape was a tall Albino policeman. As Vinnie tried to duck underneath the policeman barked:

"You can't come through here, Vinnie. "There's been an accident."

"Who are you?" Vinnie asked. "I know the local policemen and I've never seen you before and how do you know my name?"

"Now just run along sonny," the policeman said contemptuously.

"I hate it when adults treat me like a child." Vinnie protested.

"You are a child," said the policeman. "And I'm faster, smarter and better looking."

"Being small can sometimes be an advantage," Vinnie muttered.

Vinnie tried once again to slip underneath the protective tape but the Albino policeman was too fast for him. He took off his sunglasses. Underneath flashed a pair of clear blue eyes, as blue as the sea.

"I don't think that's a good idea do you?" said the policeman opening his jacket. "Step away from the barrier." Vinnie could see the policeman was wearing a gun and although he was frightened, he was angry too.

"Since when do Irish policeman wear guns?" Vinnie asked loudly enough for the crowd beside him to take notice. "Let me see your badge."

As he was about to reply, a message came through on the policeman's walky-talky.

"You can go through now," the policeman said removing the protective tape. Vinnie rushed round the corner to the grotto but Maria was not there.

End Chapter Thirteen

Chapter Fourteen

As Vinnie sat by the grotto he knew something was horribly wrong and he spontaneously burst into tears. He had tried calling Maria's phone ten times, but he got no reply. Maria asked him repeatedly not to be late and he had let her down.

He peered up at the statue of the Virgin Mary in the grotto, which had been rededicated to the people of Tarbert in 2008, looking for a sign, but none was forthcoming, so he rang Helen.

"I know Maria and you had a fight. Whatever she said to you, forget about it for now. She's missing and we need to track her down. I was supposed to meet her at the grotto at 3, she was most insistent, but when I got there she was gone."

"Did you see anything unusual?"

"A policeman I've never seen before stopped me getting through. He said there had been an accident. He was an albino."

"There were two of them in the church this morning. Do you think we should tell the local police?" said Helen.

"No," Vinnie replied firmly. ""How can we explain all this to the local police: messages from beyond the grave, Laertes, clairvoyants, they'll think we're crackers. We're on our own."

"I don't think so," said Helen. "We'll tell Mr Lyons. He'll know what to do."

****

"I'm going to make a call," said a concerned Spencer Lyons after Helen and Vinnie had explained everything. He took the clairvoyant's business card out of his desk drawer.

"Good to hear from you again Spencer," said the voice at the other end of the line. "Put me on speakerphone so Helen and Vinnie can listen in."

"Maria is missing, we think she's been kidnapped," Spencer blurted out hurriedly. "She told Vinnie Laertes took the oath of Namartis last night. What does it mean?"

"It means he has called on the spirits to enter the real world to capture Maria. You would call it kidnapping. Under the oath of Namartis no harm can come to Maria, so she is safe. She will just be held for five more days until the 30 days is up, and then her powers will disappear. Your daughter is safe for now and will not be harmed in any way. But if you try and rescue her and are unsuccessful, then you are all in danger."

"Why would they kidnap her?"

"It's been confirmed in our files. Maria is one of the six and Laertes wants to break the circle."

"If that is her destiny then we must try and save her." Spencer said.

"Be careful and good luck," said the voice at the end of the phone before hanging up.

"I'd better call mum, she'll be worried sick about me," said Vinnie and then suddenly he punched the air. "Mum, that's the answer!"

"What are you talking about?" Helen asked.

"My mom always wants to know where I am. You know how paranoid she is I'll go missing? She insisted I get a built-in GPS feature in this," he said holding up his phone. "There's one on my old phone too, the one I gave to Maria for her birthday."

"What's a GSP device?" Spencer asked.

"A GPS device can track Vinnie's phone and tell his mom where Vinnie is," Helen replied breathlessly. "So if it's on your old phone it might be able to tell us where Maria is?"

Vinnie nodded.

"It's a clever piece of software which uses twenty eight satellites to triangulate the exact geolocation of the device," he said.

When he saw Spencer's blank expression, he added: "we just need access to a computer so we can check and see."

"You can use mine," Spencer said and he gestured to his computer in the corner of his study. "Does it work if the phone is switched off or someone has taken the battery out?"

"It may give us her last known location or it might say 'location unavailable'," Vinnie replied, sitting down at the desk. "One time my mom tried to find me when I had my phone switched off. When it said I was at a 'location unavailable' she went as mad as a hatter. She thought I had found a way of hiding from her. Now let's see if we can locate you, Maria."

Vinnie's fingers whirred across the keyboard and in a matter of seconds the computer was searching for his old phone.

"It can't be," Vinnie said suddenly.

"What?" implored Spencer and Helen at the same time. "Is her phone on?"

Vinnie nodded.

"So where is Maria?"

"According to the computer she's in Besborough House, in Killimer in County Clare, 130 kilometres from here."

End Chapter Fourteen

Chapter Fifteen

"I've seen this place before," said Helen, looking at the photo on the internet. "When Maria was drawing the picture of Laertes, this house was in the background. I'm sure of it!"

Helen ran to Maria's bedroom and searched her desk before discovering the sketch. She rushed back to the computer room to show Vinnie and Spencer.

"That's it all right," said Vinnie. "See how the trees seem to be protecting the house."

"Or attacking it," said Spencer.

"What will we do?" Helen asked.

"Tell your parents you are coming on an adventure with me tomorrow," Spencer replied. "They can ring me on my mobile if they like. I'll take you both across the ferry on a trip to Killimer. Be here tomorrow morning at 9 am, that is if you are both up for a rescue mission?"

"You bet," Helen and Vinnie said together.

The following morning Spencer pulled the hearse out of the driveway and Helen and Vinnie clambered inside.

"You seem to be a good deal cheerier today Mr. Lyons," said Vinnie.

"It helped when I heard Maria is safe and won't be hurt, but I still think we should try and rescue her."

"You've got a coffin in the back of the hearse," said Helen. "Is there a..?"

"No way," Spencer smiled. "The coffin is empty. But there are some benefits to having it there," said Spencer, as what little traffic there was moved to the side of the road to let the hearse pass. Many people stood with their heads bowed and their hats off.

In the queue for the ferry the ticket collector asked:

"How many of you are there," he said, looking first at the passengers and then at the coffin in the back.

"One adult and two children," said Spencer.

"No problem," he said handing Spencer the tickets. "Sorry for your loss."

They boarded the Shannon Dolphin, a short car ferry journey across the Shannon Estuary and minutes later the vessel set sail.

"Did you know the cliffs of Moher over there are home to 30,000 nesting seabirds?" said Vinnie. "We might even see a puffin!"

"Fascinating," Helen replied, sarcastically.

"Maria was drawn to that house as a young child," Spencer said, pointing to Besborough House when they were half way across. "She used to stand here and look at it whenever we crossed on the ferry. I never realised it had any real significance until now."

"I remember her telling me when you crossed the ferry you would get to another world, with exciting new people and great things to do," Helen added.

"It does look a little like another world from here," said Vinnie, admiring the natural rugged beauty of west Clare. "Look, there's even a dolphin swimming alongside the boat."

Spencer and Helen rushed over to see. It was almost as if the dolphin was urging them to hurry as wave by wave Besborough House loomed nearer and nearer.

It was only a five minute drive from the ferry to Besborough House. There was a large padlock on the front gate and a sign saying 'closed for renovations'.

"I might have something in the back of the hearse which can help," said Spencer. While he was rummaging around in the boot, Helen took a couple of hairpins from the plaits in the back of her head.

"I saw this in a movie," Helen said. "You bend a hairpin about 90 degrees apart and then take the rubber bit off. Twist half into a small handle. Use the second hairpin as the pick," she said putting both hairpins into the lock. After a little twisting and much grimacing, the lock sprung open.

"Mr Lyons, it's sorted," Vinnie called and a surprised Spencer Lyons closed the boot of the hearse and rejoined the children.

"No security cameras," said a relieved Vinnie as they walked up the long driveway to the house.

As they got nearer, they spotted the two albino policemen standing guard at the front door.

"Wait here both of you," Vinnie ordered firmly, and he walked purposefully towards the house.

As he did so, one of the albino policemen started to walk towards him.

"Nice to see you again sonny," said the policeman. "It took some smarts to be able to track us down. Well done. But tell me, why shouldn't I just shoot you and your friends where you stand?"

"Because we have unfinished business, remember?" said Vinnie. "*I'm faster, smarter, better looking,*" he said, mimicking the policeman's voice. "It's time for you to prove it."

"It should be easy," said the policeman. "I can run faster than anyone on this planet and I can tap into the computers around the world so my brain has limitless potential. I am simply superior to you in every way."

"This is why I challenge you to a game of rock, paper, scissors," said Vinnie triumphantly. "Best out of three wins. Win and you can shoot all of us, having proved you are indeed superior. Lose and you and your friend," said Vinnie, pointing to the other policeman, "let us inside the house. Then both of you sit on the grass playing pat-a-cake for an hour."

"Also known ick-ack-ock and roshambo, rock-paper-scissors is a game for two people, where players use their hand to make one of three shapes," said the policeman in a monotone voice. "Rock beats scissors, scissors beats paper and paper beats rock. If both players choose the same shape, the game is a draw."

"You've got it," smiled Vinnie who beckoned Spencer and Helen towards him to explain what was happening.

"Are you mad?" Helen said. "If the policeman can access all the computers in the world, he will also pick the best strategy to win the game. They might as well shoot us now."

"Trust me," said Vinnie. "I have a plan."

Both Vinnie and the policeman stood side by side with Helen acting as referee.

"I will let you in on a secret," said Vinnie to the policeman. "The reason I am so confident of winning is because I learned the best strategy for this game from a rock-paper-scissors tournament at Zhejiang University in China."

"Accessing data," said the policeman and moments later he smiled broadly at Vinnie.

"Let's have one practice round to begin," said the policeman.

"One-two-three go!" said Helen. The policeman had a scissors while Vinnie showed a rock.

"I win," said Vinnie, "you see I told you I was a born winner."

"Now we'll see if you can win when it counts," said the policeman. He whispered under his breath: "Optimal metastrategy selected."

"One-two-three go!" said Helen and the policeman confidently chose paper, but Vinnie had changed from a rock and had chosen a scissors."

"Yesssssssss, one-nil," Vinnie cheered.

"Accessing frequency analysis databanks," the policeman mumbled.

"Next round. One-two-three go!" said Helen. This time the policeman chose rock, but Vinnie had switched to paper."

"Winner, winner, winner," Vinnie shouted triumphantly.

"Now I trust you will keep your word?" Helen insisted.

"We have indeed been defeated by a superior being," said the policeman, hanging his head in shame.

"How did you manage to defeat our blue-eyed friend?" Spencer enquired as the policeman unlocked the front door of Besborough House.

"It's down to collective cyclical motions," Vinnie said and when Spencer looked back at him blankly, he added:

"The Zhejiang University trial showed that winners stick with the winning formula, so if rock wins, they choose it again. Once I knew he knew what my strategy was, I was able to trap him!"

"Thanks for clearing it up for me," said Spencer who still looked confused.

He let Helen and Vinnie enter the house before watching the two policemen sit down on the grass with their arms folded.

End Chapter Fifteen

Chapter Sixteen

Helen, Vinnie and Maria threw open the doors to the grand hall and they slammed behind them. Sitting in the centre of the room was Maria in a cage. It seemed to be protected by beams of light.

"Got here OK?" Maria said casually.

Her father began to run towards her.

"Stop Dad," Maria urged. "Touch the cage and an electric charge will run through your body and you will be killed where you stand."

"What are we to do?" Spencer implored.

Vinnie was already looking round the room open-mouthed. On three of the walls were a series of oddly-shaped clocks and a fob watch, with ants scurrying across it, which looked uncannily real. There was also a giant dead tree painted on another wall with some cliffs in the background and a metal bar in the distance.

"It's a room dedicated to the 'Persistence of Memory' by Salvador Dali, the painting Ms Kearns showed us in class," said Maria. "I've got a lot more out of it looking at it than I did in class. There's a red button over there beside the only working clock. I'm guessing the secret is to set the hands of the clock to the right time and the cage will open."

"You're right," said Vinnie, looking closely at the clock. "But you only have ten seconds to set the right time. If you don't, it will shoot out a burst of electricity which will kill us all."

"Can't we find the picture on the internet?"

"There's no mobile phone coverage in here," said Vinnie peering at his iphone. "And the doors to the hall are electronically sealed shut. We can't escape unless we solve the puzzle."

"I'm afraid I've never seen this painting before," Spencer said. "Maria, what do you remember when you saw it first?"

"The story about Dali and the cheese," said Maria. "When I got home I looked at the painting on the internet, but I only noticed the two clocks which didn't have the time set. I'm drawn to the unusual and don't pay attention to the ordinary. What were you thinking of when you saw the picture, Vinnie?"

"I was thinking how awesome it would be for time to stand still. I would sit beside the dead tree singing 'New York, New York' and the crowds would cheer as the tree began to flower and come back to life."

"Helen can you be any more helpful?" Spencer asked in bewilderment.

"I hardly looked at the painting. But I remember listening to what the other children saw and thinking how different eyes see different things."

She paused before continuing.

"Someone asked why the tree was dead and someone else talked about ants on the watch. I also remember thinking how lucky it is I live close to the school. Because poor old Paula has to get up at the crack of dawn to be here."

Helen eyes began to sparkle as she realised she had solved the conundrum.

"Paula said the clock was set for the time she hated most in the morning, the time she gets up every school day, five to seven," Helen declared triumphantly.

"Are you sure?" said Spencer. "Sure enough to risk 1,000,000 volts through our bodies?"

"It's not the voltage, it's the current which kills you," Vinnie corrected.

Spencer rolled his eyes to heaven.

"Helen, we trust you," said Maria. "If you believe it is five to seven, go for it."

Helen stepped forward and started to move the hands of the clock and as she did so, lights started to flash and a voice started to count down: "ten, nine, eight, seven."

"Hurry," said Maria.

"Six, five, four," the countdown continued.

"Press the red button when you are done." Spencer urged.

"I know, I know," said Helen.

"Three, two."

Helen reached out with her right hand and pressed the button.

The laser beams flickered for a moment and the bars to the cage lifted. Helen, Vinnie and Spencer ran towards Maria and all four of them embraced.

"Let's get out of here," said Spencer and they flung open the front door and started to run down the driveway.

As they climbed into the hearse, they heard the two policemen in the background singing:

'Pat-a-cake, pat-a-cake, baker's man.

Bake me a cake as fast as you can;

Pat it and shape it and mark it with "B",

And bake it in the oven for baby and me'

End Chapter Sixteen

Chapter Seventeen

"I know you both think my Dad hits me."

"Look Helen, I wanted to apologise for..." began Maria, but Helen held her finger out to silence Maria.

"Just listen," she insisted. "I only want to talk about this once. It's not Dad who hits me. It's mum. My dad can't handle it, so he goes out drinking. And every time I get hit, Dad buys me something to ease his guilt and shame. But today it ends. I will speak to my Dad and together we will make sure mum gets help. If I need you, I will call, but I would prefer if you kept this to yourselves."

Without saying a word, Maria put her arms round her best friend.

As the ferry pulled away from the shore towards home, the adrenalin began to drain from their bodies. Spencer's eyes had heavy rings around them and Helen and Vinnie were both fast asleep in the back of the hearse.

"Dad someone has died in the last couple of days?" Maria asked.

"Yes, I finished doing the embalming last night, but..."

"No buts," said Maria. "We've only got four days left. I know whoever it is has a dying wish. They had their hands extended towards me and their eyes were open. So I plan to put my hands on them later today and see what their wish is. Now I'm exhausted, so I'm just going to close my eyes for a few moments."

Half an hour later Spencer arrived home. He glanced across the road at the gloomy graveyard and the stern church as he parked up. With the hint of moonlight and dark shadows it looked to Spencer like a good setting for a horror movie.

He smiled to himself as he carried each of the children in turn, who were all asleep into his bungalow. He put Maria on top of her bed and put a blanket over her. Then he carried Helen into the spare bedroom and finally he made a bed for Vinnie on the couch.

It was eight hours later before they rose from their slumber and Maria was angry her father had not woken her earlier.

"We have lost precious time which we could have been using to work on the last wish." Maria said.

"Please don't use this body," Spencer urged. "I don't think you realise this man has..."

"Is there someone else in the embalming room?" Maria interrupted.

"No," her father replied meekly.

"Then we have no choice, we can't wait around for someone else, we've got to use this person," Maria said, as they looked down at the body.

Helen and Vinnie seemed a bit more hesitant.

"I recognise him from somewhere. Is he a celebrity?" Helen asked.

"I think he was in the papers or on the news." Vinnie replied.

"We have no time for dilly dallying," said Maria and she raised her arms aloft confidently. She placed them deep into the man's chest.

As the 'meep meep' of the text sounded, the corners of the dead man's mouth almost seemed to turn up into a flicker of a smile.

"I've got a bad feeling about this," said Helen.

"I've been trying to tell you," Spencer said. "It's William Mullins. His son Mark is in your school. William died in a car accident after being released last week from prison for murder."

Maria bit her lip.

"It's possible his last wish is something good, isn't it?" she said despairingly. "Maybe he wants to make amends?"

"There's only one way to find out," Helen replied and Maria pressed 'play' on her mobile phone.

On screen they saw the inside of a photo booth. But this time the shadowy figure sat down in front of the camera so that Spencer and the children could see his face clearly.

"How delicious," he said in a deep rasping voice. "I'm surprised to hear from you Maria. I hear you were mean to my son. That's not very nice. But now you have got in touch, I will tell you what I want."

He leaned forward and spoke slowly and clearly into the camera.

"For my last wish, I want you to take my..."

-ends-

ABOUT THE AUTHOR

Anthony Garvey has over 25 years experience working in international public relations, ranging from technology and telecommunication blue chips to educational and local government organisations. He spent 9 years as Head of PR for Psion plc as it evolved from a start-up to a FTSE100 company. In 2001, Anthony returned to Ireland where he established Quinn Garvey PR which provides public relations and marketing services to small businesses in Ireland and the UK. Anthony is married with two young sons, Zachary and Samuel and lives with his wife Siobhan in Tralee, in County Kerry. This is Anthony's second published work. His first, the Dark Green Book of Dreams was published in December 2013. This book is the first in a series of children's books, the second of which will be ready for publication later in 2016.

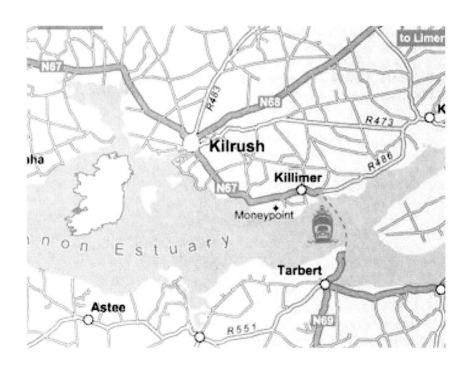

Tarbert (County Kerry) and Killimer (County Clare)